RETURN OF
ZOMBERT

RETURN OF
ZOMBERT

Kara LaReau

illustrated by Ryan Andrews

CANDLEWICK PRESS

Text copyright © 2021 by Kara LaReau
Illustrations copyright © 2021 by Ryan Andrews

First edition 2021

Library of Congress Catalog Card Number pending
ISBN 978-1-5362-0107-9

21 22 23 24 25 26 LBM 10 9 8 7 6 5 4 3 2 1

Printed in Melrose Park, IL, USA

This book was typeset in ITC Mendoza Roman.
The illustrations were done digitally.

Candlewick Press
99 Dover Street
Somerville, Massachusetts 02144

www.candlewick.com

A JUNIOR LIBRARY GUILD SELECTION

For Sugar
KL

For Bristow and Dakota
RA

CHAPTER ONE

In a certain corporate headquarters on the edge of town, all was quiet. Even the animals in the research and development lab were quiet. But that's because they were sedated.

In the executive suite, far from the research and development lab, on the top floor of that corporate headquarters, one animal wasn't sedated—it was sitting on the desk, and it was gulping eagerly.

"This one is special," the Big Boss said, feeding it a handful of raw meat.

"That's what you said about Y-91," Kari said. That animal had been nothing but trouble for them. Just when it looked like they were about to make a breakthrough in their research, it escaped the lab— and it was still on the loose, somehow evading them at every turn. Even now, thinking about it made Kari angry.

"Y-91 had potential, but it also had limits," the Big Boss said. "Y-92 has surpassed our every expectation."

Greg appeared behind them. He seemed out of breath.

"You're late," Kari said. Never in her life had she been late for anything. How was it that Greg got away with being such a slacker? No matter how hard Kari worked, it was clear he was the Big Boss's favorite.

"I've been on an assignment, remember?" Greg said.

"And how is that assignment proceeding?" the Big Boss asked.

"Mellie Gore definitely has contact with Y-91," Greg said. "She talks about it all the time."

"We should have apprehended the animal when the Gore girl brought it to YummCo Animal Pals for a checkup," Kari said. "We told the staff there to call us as soon as they saw a cat matching Y-91's description."

"You told them to look for a cat missing most of its fur," Greg reminded her. "The cat she brought in had a full, glossy coat."

"How was I to know its regeneration powers had kicked in so quickly?" Kari said, her face reddening. "In any case, the vet called us as soon as the bloodwork came back looking suspicious."

"Too late for it to help us," Greg said.

"The bloodwork has helped us in other ways," Kari said.

"I've heard enough of your past mistakes," the Big Boss said, pounding a fist on the desk. "What are we doing *now*?"

"I had the Gore house searched while the family was out. Our team found nothing," Kari reminded the Big Boss.

"I don't think it lives in the house, not all the time anyway," Greg said. "But it does seem to trust her.

And our cyber team's hack of her phone shows photos of her with Y-91 on more than a few occasions."

Greg thought he was so cool ever since the Big Boss put him in charge of the "cyber team." So what if he'd used an e-mail from a Lost Pet sign to track down the Gore girl through her friend? It was just a lucky break. Kari almost missed Walter, the scientist Greg had replaced. At least Walter had been brilliant, someone she actually respected. Too bad he was dead now.

"The bloodwork we were able to access through the system at YummCo Animal Pals has yielded some important findings. But we need to bring in Y-91 for further examination," Kari said. "There's a lot we still don't know about how this formula works."

"The new version we've created shows promise," the Big Boss said.

"If that's true, do we even *need* Y-91 anymore?" Greg asked.

"We're closer to our goal with the original formula—though we can't know for sure until we do further experiments," Kari said.

"And Y-91 is evidence of our experiments. We can't have that evidence roaming around," the Big Boss said, giving the animal another handful of meat. It ate voraciously.

"Why don't we have YummCo Animal Pals contact the Gore girl and tell her there's something wrong with the animal?" Kari suggested. "We can tell her it needs further testing."

"Too suspicious. I know all too well what girls like Mellie Gore are like at that age, too smart for their own good. No, we need something clever. She and the cat need to be brought out together, out in public," the Big Boss said. "Somewhere they're vulnerable."

"Why can't we just show up at her house and take the cat?" Greg asked. "It's our property, after all."

Kari sighed. Greg's mind seemed like it was enveloped in a layer of bubble wrap.

"Because YummCo isn't supposed to be testing its products on animals," she reminded him. "We've made that pledge on every one of our products. It would be a PR nightmare if it came out that we lied. Trust is everything."

"I get it. The last thing we want to do is parade our secrets in front of the town," Greg said, looking sheepish.

"Parade? Hmm . . ." The Big Boss thought for a moment, then smiled. "What an *excellent* idea."

CHAPTER TWO

Okay, Gore Gang. Who wants spaghetti carbonara?" my dad asked.

"Me! Me-me-me-me-me!" Emmett and Ezra cried, clapping.

"Me too," I said. Though I knew, as always, I'd need to wait my turn.

My mom and dad had been better about filming at the table and allowing for family time that wasn't on camera. But they'd just converted their *Family, Food, and Fun* blog into a YummTube online channel, after they'd received a big sponsorship from YummCo Foods; it came with new YummPhones for us and a new YummBook laptop for my parents. The PR department there even talked to my parents about turning their videos into a book. So while my dad was hard at work developing recipes, my mom was doing whatever she could to "increase their fan base."

"How's Bert?" my dad asked, finally scooping some spaghetti carbonara onto my plate. He knows exactly how much to give me, which is a lot, since spaghetti carbonara is one of my favorites. Anything with bacon is my favorite, actually.

"Great," I said. Thanks to my parents, I'd finally been able to take Bert to YummCo Animal Pals for a checkup, and according to his bloodwork, he was one of the healthiest cats the vet had ever seen. Still, Bert didn't love being poked and prodded on the metal table; he growled the whole time and tried to scratch the vet and her assistant, so they had to put on special gloves to handle him. But I couldn't blame him since I don't love going to the doctor, either. On the upside, getting a clean bill of health from the vet meant that Bert was officially, finally part of our family.

"And how are you doing with paying off our loan?" my mom asked, raising her eyebrows.

"It's . . . taking way longer than I thought," I admitted. My parents had given me the money for Bert's vet visit, but they expected me to pay it back ASAP; they said they were trying to teach me "fiscal responsibility." They helped me put an odd-jobs notice on our neighborhood message board, but so far I'd only gotten calls to rake leaves and fold laundry, neither of which paid very much.

"Bringing home the bacon isn't easy," Dad said.

"And Bert doesn't even like bacon," I said. He really only liked killing his own food, and even then, he just preferred the heads of his prey.

"That reminds me," my mom said. "On my way to the park with the twins this morning, I saw Mrs. Witt. She says she has some yard work for you to do."

"You mean the Candy Witch?" I asked.

My mom sighed. "You need to stop calling her that," she said. "Her name is Candy *Witt*."

"That's what all the kids call her," I said. "But she does give out the best treats on Halloween. I guess I can go and rake her leaves or whatever."

"It's nice that you'll be helping her out," my dad said.

"It's nice that she'll be *paying* me," I reminded him.

"I'm sure it's been hard for her since Mr. Witt passed away," Mom said.

My dad looked at the twins' plates. "If you don't finish, you won't get dessert. And tonight we're having brownie sundaes, with my all-time fave: mint chocolate chip ice cream!"

"I think you'd eat mint chocolate chip ice cream for every meal if you could," my mom said.

"You might be right," my dad said, giving her a wink.

"Sundaes!" said Emmett. "Wif whipped cream?"

"And a chair-wee on top?" asked Ezra.

"You got it," said Dad.

After dinner, I took my brownie sundae up to my room, where Bert was waiting for me, curled up on my bed. We had a little routine now where I let him into the house in the morning before I left for school, and he'd nap in my room until I got home. Then we'd hang out together before the sun went down, which was his time for dinner. Though his dinner involved hunting and beheading instead of cooking.

"How are you?" I asked, scratching him gently behind his good ear. He purred a little, which I took as a good sign.

He was looking a lot better than he had a month ago, when I first found him in a recycling barrel outside the YummCo Foods factory. Back then he was just skin and bones. Now he'd filled out a lot, his gray

fur was growing in thick and shiny, and his yellow eyes were bright. He actually seemed almost . . . normal. But I knew the truth: Bert wasn't like other cats. He was smart—and unusual, just like me.

"Don't worry," I said. "I'm going to find a way to pay back my parents soon. Then we'll have even more time to hang out."

I leaned in close.

"I'm just glad you're part of our family officially now," I whispered.

Bert looked at me and blinked, which is what cats do when they really like you. I blinked back.

CHAPTER THREE

He'd had a dream about his mother.

It was the last time he'd seen her, on a cold night the winter before. He and his brother and sister were not much older than kittens, but they no longer craved their mother's milk. They were hungry for food, and there was none to be found.

They slept in an abandoned den their mother had discovered, beneath the tallest pine tree in the forest. The den smelled faintly of fox musk, but it was big enough for all of them, and it was warm. They huddled together, he and his brother and sister, as their mother went out into the cold to find them something to eat.

"I'll be back," she'd told them. "Stay here, and stay together."

She'd never returned. The night turned to day, and then to night again, before he and his siblings felt brave enough to venture out into the forest to find her. They'd walked together until they got lost and hid in a pile of leaves underneath a shrub.

That's when the Rough Hands had found them and brought them to the Cold Place and put them all in cages. Huddled there under the shrub with his brother and sister was the last time he'd felt their warmth, or had any hope that they'd survive together. When he woke up on the girl's bed where he slept now, he almost thought he could feel them next to him.

He stalked through the woods now with two things in mind: he needed to eat, and he needed to plan.

First things first. He stopped, sniffing the air. Something juicy was hiding, just beneath that pile of leaves. When his hunger came to him, it was almost painful, like a stabbing deep inside and a pounding in his brain. Once he ate, he'd feel stronger—and lighter, almost as if he could fly. And his brain would start buzzing. Lately, he'd been remembering and understanding more and more, as if pieces were being connected inside his head.

Whatever was rustling beneath the leaves, he could sense its heartbeat, so fast, so anxious. He would make it quick with this one, put it out of its misery. He did enjoy playing with his prey, but lately he was distracted by something more important: revenge.

He thought back to the Cold Place, where he

spent his time in a cage, or held down on a metal table as the Rough Hands pricked and poked him with even colder, sharper things. The eyes of those who tended to him were unfeeling, especially the One who had eyes like ice and the roughest hands. The other animals were afraid of the One, and the other humans were, too. The One had told the Rough Hands to give him something that made him sick and weak. If he hadn't escaped when he did, he would have died. But he hadn't wanted to leave alone. He wished he could have brought others with him. His brother, even weaker than he was, who cried in his cage each night until he'd been taken away. His sister, who lasted only a few days in the Cold Place before she succumbed to whatever the Rough Hands had done to her.

The thing under the leaves began to stir. A small brown-furred thing with a stripe down its back, big brown eyes filled with fear.

You will do nicely, he thought, ready to pounce.

CHAPTER FOUR

I thought my mom said you had yard work for me," I said.

"Well, technically, this shed *is* in the yard," Mrs. Witt said. She brushed a silvery cobweb away from her equally silvery hair.

I coughed. There were cobwebs everywhere, and dust. But more than anything, there were papers—diagrams and charts and scribbled formulas on the tables and tacked to the walls. And there were all sorts of lab equipment, including a microscope nicer than any I'd seen in my *KidScience!* catalog.

"This was my husband's workshop," Mrs. Witt explained.

"You said he worked for YummCo."

"They hired him after they bought our business," Mrs. Witt said. "Walter and I used to have our own candy company, Witts Confectionery."

"You owned a *candy company?*" I said. It sounded like the best job ever, maybe even better than being a scientist, which was what I wanted to be.

"Yep, I was Candy who made candy. Walter used to say I finally lived up to my name," Mrs. Witt said, chuckling. "He had a PhD in chemistry, so he helped me come up with all sorts of concoctions. And then YummCo came to town and made us an offer we couldn't refuse, for the business and all our recipes, and a job for Walter in their lab."

"Mr. Witt was a chemist?" I said. I always thought the Witts were just old people who lived down the street from us and gave out the best candy on Halloween.

"We both studied chemistry in college," Mrs. Witt said. "That's where we met. Then we got married and had Wally, our son. Walter went on to get his PhD and while I stayed home with Wally, I started making little candies, just for fun. Then Walter started helping me on the weekends; that's when things really took off. We had a nice storefront on Main Street and a factory on the edge of town."

She brushed off a photo in a thick frame on one of the walls and showed it to me. Mr. and Mrs. Witt looked much younger; they were standing in front of a tall brick building with lots of windows. A plaque on the frame read THE GIFT THAT KEEPS ON GIVING.

THE GIFT THAT KEEPS ON GIVING

"You both look so happy here," I said.

"It was one of the happiest days of our lives together. This was the grand opening of the Witts Confectionery factory. We'd put everything we had into making that dream come true," Mrs. Witt explained. "And it was our anniversary—Walter and

I used to joke that this was the best anniversary gift we could have given to each other. He called our little factory 'the gift that keeps on giving.'"

"Wait," I said, leaning in. "This looks familiar."

"It should. It's where YummCo corporate head-quarters is now. They just painted the whole thing white," Mrs. Witt said. "And added the campus around it, with their own factory buildings."

She showed me another frame, containing blueprints.

"Walter and I worked closely with the architect on renovating the old Lambert Pharmaceutical building. It was so exciting back then, saving an old town landmark, working together and building our business," Mrs. Witt said.

"I wish I'd known Mr. Witt," I said. "Science is my favorite subject."

"It's my favorite, too," Mrs. Witt said. "I'll talk with you about it whenever you like. It always makes me think of Walter."

"So . . . where do you want me to start?" I asked.

Mrs. Witt pulled out some boxes. "I haven't been able to come out here since Walter died. It makes me too sad. But I don't want his things to sit out here and get dusty and moldy, or worse. A few months back, someone actually tried to break in here—good thing Walter's alarm system was still activated."

"Why would someone want to break in here?" I asked, looking around again at the dusty clutter.

"You'd be surprised what some people consider valuable," Mrs. Witt said. "Of course, everything here is valuable to me because it all feels like parts of Walter. I need a fresh perspective, and your mom said you were looking for jobs in the neighborhood and that you liked science. So I thought we could go through everything together so I can decide what to keep and what to donate to the high school."

A lab coat and goggles hung on pegs next to the shed door. "Were these Mr. Witt's?"

"They were. I'll probably give them to Wally," Mrs. Witt said. She took them down and gave them a shake.

We both coughed. And then Mrs. Witt laughed.

"I guess I've put this off long enough," she said. "Where should we start?"

"Maybe with some dusting," I suggested.

CHAPTER FIVE

W hat happened to you?" Danny asked when I finally got to his apartment that afternoon.

"Mrs. Witt," I said, brushing cobwebs off my arm. "She said she had yard work for me to do. I didn't expect I'd end up cleaning out her husband's workshop."

"Workshop?" Danny said. "Find anything good in there?"

"Yeah, but it's like no one's been in there for a hundred years. We spent all morning just dusting and packing everything up." It had taken extra long because we had to be so careful—Mrs. Witt said some of the equipment might still have chemical residue.

She had us both wear respirators and gloves while we worked and loaded the test tubes, pipettes, and petri dishes into Mr. Witt's special laboratory dishwasher.

"Sounds like it would be an awesome place to film," Danny said. He's always making horror movies, which he posts on his online channel, Hurlvision.

"Good luck with that. I could barely fit, with all the stuff crammed in there," I said.

"Did the Candy Witch give you anything else?" Danny raised his eyebrows.

"Yes," I said, rolling my eyes. "But let's not call her that anymore. Mrs. Witt's a really nice old lady. And she knows about science."

I rummaged around in my coveralls pocket and took out the bag Mrs. Witt gave me. I gave one candy to Danny and took one for myself.

"This tastes like a YummCo Fizzer, only . . . better," he said.

I looked at the wrapper. It said WITTS CONFECTIONERY.

"That's because this was made by the Witts before YummCo bought their company," I said. "I bet YummCo changed the recipe."

"Big mistake," Danny said.

"I wish YummCo Animal Pals was hiring," I said. "I could have worked there in exchange for free checkups and shots for Bert. And I could have learned about animals."

"Mmm . . . this candy is super fizzy," Danny said. "Think you could get Mrs. Witt to give you more?"

I handed Danny the bag. "I think this job is working out better for you than me," I said. "Maybe you need to work for Mrs. Witt."

"No thanks," Danny said. "Though it would be another excuse for me to get out of the apartment so I don't have to be around my mom and her *boyfriend*."

"You have to admit, she seems a lot happier these days," I said.

Danny sighed. He knew I was right. But the last guy his mom was with was Danny's dad, who turned out to be a total jerk, so I can see why he'd be suspicious of anyone new and why he wouldn't want to share anything with this new guy. But he really seemed to like Ms. Hurley. And he was nice to Danny and me. It was like he was really listening to us when we talked, like he actually found us interesting.

A few minutes later, we heard the lock and the deadbolt on the apartment door, and it opened.

"Honey, we're home!" Ms. Hurley's voice called out brightly.

Danny took a deep breath. "How was the movie?" he asked.

"So romantic," Ms. Hurley said, sighing. "Didn't you think so?"

She turned to Greg, the new boyfriend.

"Totally," he said. He reached into his jacket pocket and pulled out a half-eaten bag of YummCo Fizzers. "Your mom said you'd want the rest of these, buddy."

"Thanks, but Mellie just brought me some candy," Danny said. "If I eat any more I'll get cavities."

"Since when are you worried about the dentist?" Ms. Hurley said.

"I'll eat one," I said. Danny was right; the YummCo Fizzers really weren't as good as the Witts'. "So . . . anything interesting happening at work?"

In addition to being nice, Greg also happened to work in the research and development lab at YummCo, which sounded like it would be the most interesting job in the world. Well, the second-most interesting, compared to owning a candy company.

"One project I'm working on is starting to show some real results," Greg said, raising an eyebrow. "But you know I can't talk about it."

"Because you signed a confidentiality agreement," I said. "Right."

"How's your cat?" Greg asked, sitting in the chair next to me. "What was its name? Bob?"

"Bert. His name is Bert," I said. "He's good. I just wish I had more time to spend with him. I owe my parents for his vet bill, so I've been working to pay them back."

"Mellie's been doing odd jobs around the neighborhood," Ms. Hurley explained.

"Huh," Greg said. He pulled a flyer out of his jacket pocket and handed it to me. "Well, it just so happens I saw this at work and thought of you. Maybe it will help?"

The flyer promoted the Lambert Harvest Festival, sponsored by YummCo.

"Since when has our town had a Harvest Festival?" Danny asked.

"I think it's nice that YummCo always finds ways to give something to the community," Ms. Hurley said. "They're going to have games, rides, food, and even a *parade*."

"And check out this part." Greg pointed to the bottom of the flyer. I read it and looked at Danny.

LAMBERT HARVEST FESTIVAL

SPONSORED BY YUMMCO!

GAMES!
FOOD!

DON'T MISS THE
MEET·N·GREET
WITH MR. YUMM
HIMSELF!

1ST ANNUAL BEST PET CONTEST $200⁰⁰ PRIZE!!

"They're holding a Best Pet Contest," I said.

"The winning pet and its owner will get to ride in the Harvest Parade on the YummCo Foods float with Mr. Yumm," Ms. Hurley said. Mr. Yumm was the CEO of YummCo Foods, and Ms. Hurley the receptionist at their corporate headquarters here in Lambert.

"And they'll get *two hundred dollars*," I said. "That will more than pay for Bert's vet visit!"

"Um . . . Bert is great and all. But do you think he's really the 'Best Pet' in Lambert?" Danny asked.

"Of course. Bert is super smart," I reminded him. "He's not like other pets. In the best way."

"Well, I know that, and you know that," Danny said. "But how are you going to prove that to the contest judges? You know he's awesome, and I know he's awesome, but to anyone who doesn't know him, Bert does seem . . . kind of weird."

"That's exactly why we need to win," I said. "It's time we proved to everyone that weird is awesome!"

"You'll be a shoo-in if your cat is as great as you say it is," Greg said. "Just make sure you're registered before the deadline."

Oh, I'll make sure we're registered, I thought. *And I'll make sure that Bert and I win.*

CHAPTER SIX

I just received a promising report from Greg," said the Big Boss, gazing out a window of the YummCo executive suite. "He's told the Gore girl about the contest. He's confident she'll take the bait."

"Let's hope we can trust Greg's instincts," Kari said, making notes on her YummPad. "Things are going smoothly with the Harvest Festival organizing. I ordered extra food, as you requested."

"Excellent," said the Big Boss.

"Are you sure you want everything to be free?" Kari asked. "We're not going to turn a profit on this event *at all*."

The Big Boss smiled. "Trust me, let's not worry ourselves about upfront costs or profits. This is a long-term investment. It's about giving something special to Lambert."

"When you put it that way, it does make sense," Kari said. She cleared her throat.

"Is there something else?" the Big Boss asked.

Kari was nervous to bring it up, but she knew she had to.

"Y-92 is the only subject to survive our most recent round of testing," she said. She slid her YummPad across the desk.

"As I expected," said the Big Boss, skimming the research notes. "You can't make an omelet without breaking a few eggs."

"Eggs?" Kari said.

"I hope you're not letting your feelings get in the way of your work," the Big Boss said, raising an eyebrow.

"N-no, of course not," Kari said.

"The loss of a handful of expendable subjects is far outweighed by the significance of our progress on the formula. We're not creating a new ice cream flavor or trying to make our Cheezy YummCo Blasts even cheesier," the Big Boss said. "With the development of Yummconium, we're hoping to improve the human race by making it stronger, faster, smarter, healthier. For YummCo, and for the world."

The Big Boss was right again, of course. Kari never liked to lose any subjects, but their research could change everything. She couldn't wait until she could finally tell her parents about her role in YummCo's research. Finally, they'd see that she wasn't just some little lab assistant. Her sister might be a heart surgeon and her brother might be a civil rights lawyer, but Kari was on the team that would introduce Yummconium to the world. Of course, that couldn't happen until it was ready. And to be ready, the formula had to be perfect.

"Well, Y-92 has shown some of the results we'd hoped for with our previous version of the Yummconium formula: a sharp decline in vital statistics, followed by rapid regeneration, keen senses, physical prowess, enhanced memory and cognitive function, appetite only for fresh-caught prey," Kari said. "But its appetite is . . . concerning. Y-92 seems ravenous beyond anything we've seen before—we can barely sate its appetite before it's hungry again."

"Ravenous?" the Big Boss said, raising an eyebrow. "Now that is . . . concerning."

"Even more concerning: its hunger is paired with extremely aggressive behaviors," Kari added. "We keep increasing the amount of sedatives we need to use in order to handle the animal."

"That's certainly worth further examination," the Big Boss said.

"Maybe we should halt our research until we can get Y-91 back," Kari said. "As I've said before, I think we've gone too far with this round. We need to study Y-91 and see where we can make the Yummconium formula less volatile."

"We're too close to a breakthrough to stop now," the Big Boss said. "Increase your order from YummCo Animal Pals. Feel free to double or even triple the number of animals they've been sending you for our research: dogs, cats, rabbits, rats, mice . . . whatever they have. Use some of them for another round of testing and the rest to satisfy Y-92's . . . appetites."

Kari hesitated. But the Big Boss was right; a

breakthrough was just around the corner. She'd request a new shipment from the animal shelter right away.

"Hopefully we can get Y-91 back into the lab soon so we can do further testing," she said. "We want our consumers to eat products made with Yummconium and feel like better versions of themselves—not slaves to their appetites."

"Of course," the Big Boss said, closing the YummPad and sliding it across the desk.

After Kari went back to the lab, the Big Boss went to the window, which looked out onto the YummCo factory and the cemetery. The weather had been windier than usual this fall, so most of the leaves had already fallen from the trees, providing a clearer view beyond, into the town of Lambert.

The Big Boss pressed an outstretched palm against the glass and smiled. Everything was going according to plan.

CHAPTER SEVEN

Are you sure this is going to work?" Danny asked.

"Ms. Michiko said that this was the best book on cat training," I said. Ms. Michiko was the children's librarian at the YummCo Memorial Library, and she was never wrong. The book was called *Clickety-Clack: Training for Cats*, and it showed you how to use a special clicker to reinforce behavior. Unfortunately, the clicker didn't come with the book, so I had to buy it at the pet store with some of the money I'd already earned from helping Mrs. Witt.

"The book says I'm supposed to give Bert a treat when he exhibits the right behavior," I said, flipping through the pages. "Something he really enjoys eating."

"Uhh . . . animal heads?" Danny asked.

"Hmm," I said.

I went into my house. When I came out a few minutes later, Danny raised his eyebrows.

"Is that who I think it is?" he said.

"It is," I said.

I held out what was left of Mr. Peepers, my favorite childhood stuffed animal. Bert had beheaded the fuzzy yellow chick on the first night he spent in my room. Since then, it had become his favorite chew toy.

"Mr. Peepers has decided to donate his body to science," I explained. "Or at least, his head."

"Mrow," Bert said, licking his lips.

"Sounds like you're ready. Let's get to work," I said. "We're going to do three things: get you to touch a YummCo sticker with your nose, jump over something, and open a drawer."

I consulted *Clickety-Clack*. The author, Karen Clackerson, made it all sound so easy; she even trained dolphins with her method. It must work because she's now retired and living in Hawaii.

"I thought cats were supposed to be independent," Danny said.

"The book says that the cat is supposed to be treated like an equal training partner," I said. "If you want to get them to touch something, you hold the target in front of it first."

I held my hand in front of Bert. Right away, he rubbed his nose against it, so I clicked the clicker and gave him Mr. Peepers's head to gnaw on for a few seconds. When he was done, he looked up at me expectantly.

"Good job, Bert!" I said. I took away Mr. Peepers and held out my hand. "Let's try again!"

Bert did it again on the second try. *Click*. Gnaw.

He did it again on the third try. *Click*. Gnaw.

"Wow, Mellie. He really is smart," said Danny.

"Mrow!" Bert said, as if he agreed.

"I told you," I said, fishing around in my pocket for the YummCo sticker. "Now let's keep going."

But as soon as I put the sticker on my hand and held it out, Bert meowed and lay down on the grass.

"Come on, Bert. Just one more try. We're so close," I said.

He closed his eyes. It was like he wasn't listening to me at all.

"Don't you want to show the world how awesome you are?" I asked.

"You can't expect to train him in one day," Danny said.

"The Harvest Festival is *next weekend*," I reminded him. "We don't have much time."

"Remember, the book said the cat is an *equal partner*," Danny said.

I looked down at Bert. My "equal partner" had already fallen asleep. His legs were twitching. I hoped, at least, that he was having a good dream.

CHAPTER EIGHT

The first human word he'd understood was the name the girl had given him: Bert.

Every day, it seemed his brain was expanding and making connections, allowing him to understand more of the world. It was a great gift, to suddenly know so much, to feel a hunger for knowledge as much as a hunger for food. But it was frustrating not to be able to convey his knowledge to the humans.

Today, something clicked and he finally understood: the girl's name was Mellie. The boy's name was Danny.

He went along with Mellie and what she called their "training" because he trusted her, and because he owed her his life. But he could not stay focused, not when he had his own plans to think about.

He thought about the other animals, still in their cages back in the Cold Place. When he escaped, he promised he'd come back for them. He needed to save them, the way he hadn't managed to save his siblings.

He remembered his sister; she'd been the smallest of the three in their litter, but her mews had always been the loudest. She'd been all gray like him, but with white paws. She was so terrified when they were first placed in their cages, she hadn't made a sound. He'd tried to call to her, to soothe her, but the sounds of the other animals had drowned him out. Within days, she was gone.

He remembered his brother, whimpering in his

cage, so weak, so sick, from whatever the Rough Hands had given him. He knew his brother was dying, and yet there was nothing he could do. And then, in the middle of the night, the Rough Hands had taken his brother away. That was the last time they'd seen each other. It was then that Bert decided to escape, and it was then that he'd vowed revenge.

The sun coming through the window was warm on his fur, and the blankets on Mellie's bed were soft and smelled like her. He took a deep breath and allowed himself to fall asleep. He needed to rest so he'd have the energy to do what he needed to do. He dreamed of the Rough Hands and what he would do to them when he saw them again.

CHAPTER NINE

W hat's with all the cereal?" I asked. We'd been finding half-eaten boxes of YummCo Nutty Clusters and spoons and empty bowls all over Mr. Witt's workshop.

"It was Walter's favorite thing to eat while he was working," Mrs. Witt said, laughing. "He'd order it from Super YummCo by the case. The man did love his cereal."

"And he loved notebooks," I said, handing Mrs. Witt another stack of them. Mr. Witt had numbered each of their spines so he could keep track of them. I liked knowing he was so organized, like me.

"I wish Walter had lived to see all of his ideas come to life," Mrs. Witt said. "Or at least the last project he was working on; he said it was going to change everything."

"Did he like working for YummCo? I mean, before he got fired?" I asked.

"At first, he did." Mrs. Witt put the notebooks in a cardboard box. "He said everything in the research and development department was state-of-the-art. And that the new products they were designing were cutting-edge. He loved discovering new ways to make people's lives easier and better, though he couldn't tell me any specific details, of course."

"The confidentiality agreement," I said. "I've heard about that."

"Walter was really strict about it. That made it hard when things started to change. When he came home from work, he looked sad, and when I'd ask him about it, he'd just shake his head. Then, finally, he said he was going to do something about it. That was the day they fired him."

"Why?" I asked.

"They said he stole something that belonged to

the company. They call it IP, or intellectual property," she said. "Investigators came and took Walter's computer. They rifled through his research. And right after that he got sick, so I don't know if they ever found what they were looking for."

"That sounds awful," I said. I remembered what it was like when everyone thought that Bert had done something to Carl Weems's rat, but it turned out she'd just gone off to hide to have her babies. I couldn't imagine being accused of something even more serious and knowing you were innocent. Not to mention having someone come in and mess with your stuff, and even take some of it away from you.

"Maybe we've had enough cleaning for one morning," Mrs. Witt said, checking her watch. "Why don't you come in the house and pick out some candy for you and your friend? You said he likes our Witt Fizzles?"

"We *both* like them. They're better than YummCo Fizzers," I said. "Way better."

"We'd make so much more progress if you just applied yourself," I told Bert that afternoon. This was what my old piano teacher, Mr. Mathers, used to tell me. Unfortunately, it worked just as well on Bert as it had on me.

"He's just a cat," Danny reminded me through a mouthful of Witt Fizzle.

"He's not just a cat," I said. "He's *Bert*."

But even Danny wasn't really paying attention; he was filming Bert at all kinds of angles.

"What are you doing?" I asked.

"If I edit these together the right way, it's going to look super creepy," Danny explained. "I wish you could train him to run with all his teeth showing. *Return of ZomBert* needs a good chase scene."

Return of ZomBert was the second in what Danny was calling his ZomBert Trilogy. The first story got him a lot of hits on Hurlvision and showed up on Twizzle and Faceplace, which are social media sites I only know about from Danny because my parents say I'm too young to visit them. Danny says the second story in a trilogy is always the hardest to make, so I couldn't be too annoyed that he wasn't helping me.

I just wanted to show the world that Bert was more than a horror movie monster; he was an amazing pet.

At today's training session, he'd finally mastered touching the YummCo sticker on my hand. And he was doing pretty well at jumping over Emmett and Ezra's toy YummCo truck. It was opening the drawer of my jewelry box and pulling out the YummCo keychain that was the problem. He seemed to get it right the first couple of times, then he'd lose interest.

"Well, if it isn't the Weirdo Twins," a voice behind us said. I looked at Danny and sighed because I knew exactly who it was: Carl Weems. Carl lived in my neighborhood, and he was in fourth grade with me and Danny. We used to call him our archnemesis; sometimes he seemed like a bully, but most times I just felt sorry for him.

"Hey, Carl," I said.

"Hey," Danny said, with even less enthusiasm.

Carl was wearing a NASA T-shirt and baggy bright-green sweatpants. He was smiling until he saw Bert.

"Uh, is that the zombie cat?" he asked as Bert retreated under the rhododendron bush.

"His name is Bert, and he's not a zombie," I reminded him.

"He just plays one on Hurlvision," Danny added.

"What are you doing?" Carl asked. When I didn't say anything, I saw him look over at *Clickety-Clack* on the picnic table. "Wait. Are you actually trying to *train* that thing?"

"Maybe," I said.

Carl laughed, showing his gray tooth, which he got from flipping over his handlebars while trying to pop a wheelie on his bike last summer.

"I hope you're not thinking you're going to win the Best Pet Contest at the festival next weekend. Because I've got that one *locked up*," Carl said. "You've got one lazy, freaky cat. I have four *amazing* rats, so I have four chances to win."

"Sure, Carl. We'll see who's *really* amazing," I said.

"Okay, see you weirdos at school. Unless . . . you feel like going to the park or something," Carl said.

"Bert and I have more training to do," I said.

"And I'm filming," said Danny. "You actually walked right onto a live set."

"Yeah, well, whatever," said Carl. "Enjoy losing next weekend!"

"I'm sick of being called weird, like it's a bad

thing," I said once Carl had gotten on his bike and pedaled off. "It should be cool that I like science and experiments and learning stuff, and that you like horror movies."

"Carl should talk," Danny said. "He's weird, too. Remember you found out he's obsessed with outer space? And he seems *super* into those rats. Everyone is a little bit weird."

"Well, we should celebrate it, not make fun of it," I said.

I leaned down to Bert, who had fallen asleep under the rhododendron bush.

"Did you hear that?" I said. "We've got to win one for the weirdos! Are you with me?"

Bert opened one eye.

"Good," I said, holding up my clicker and Mr. Peepers's head. "Break time is *over*."

CHAPTER TEN

I t's official," Greg said. "Mellie Gore has registered the cat for the contest."

"Perfect," said the Big Boss. "You've certainly redeemed yourself on this project."

"Thank you," said Greg. Behind him, Kari wrinkled her nose. Greg's job was so easy compared to hers. She was stuck planning the entire Harvest Festival while he was going out on dates—on YummCo's dime, no less!—and hanging out with kids.

"And our plans for the festival," the Big Boss said, looking at Kari. "How are those proceeding?"

Kari was annoyed that the Big Boss kept refer-ring to it as "our plans for the festival" when she was doing all of the work and making none of the deci-sions. "I can only trust you with this special event," the Big Boss had said at the beginning. "You have the best head for details."

Of course, that part was true. And if this is what it took to get that promotion to senior lab assistant, she was willing to put up with just about anything. As senior lab assistant, she would be Greg's boss; that perk was almost better than the new title and the pay raise and pleasing her parents.

"We have everything in place. The parade floats, the games, the music. And the food," Kari said, showing the Big Boss her plans on her YummPad.

"We can't afford any mistakes," the Big Boss said. "If anything goes wrong, *heads will roll*."

"Nothing will go wrong. Unless someone else messes up," Kari said. She made sure to look at Greg.

As they left the executive suite and went back to the lab, Greg chuckled.

"You know, this project wasn't all that hard," he

admitted. "I actually like Roxanne and Danny Hurley and Mellie Gore."

Kari glared at him.

"*Never* admit that to anyone else, especially the Big Boss," Kari said. "That was a *project*. It's like the tests we do in the lab. You never let your feelings get in the way of your work."

"So I can't keep seeing Roxanne?" Greg asked.

Kari rolled her eyes.

The Big Boss watched Kari and Greg go back to the lab and waited for them to leave for the night. It was time to put the most important piece of the plan into motion.

When the Big Boss stepped into the lab, the animals immediately backed into the farthest corners of their cages. Except for the one in the cage marked Y-92. After a seemingly endless feeding session, that creature had finally fallen asleep. Now it opened one eye.

"Good evening, my pet," the Big Boss whispered. "Tomorrow's a big day for you and me. All of our *delicious* plans are about to fall into place."

The other animals shifted in their cages as the Big Boss put the finishing touches on the most recent batch of Yummconium, then headed to the factory floor with a case of the formula. Y-92 closed its eyes and settled in for the night. When it woke the next morning, it was ravenous again . . . and everything was ready.

CHAPTER ELEVEN

Everything is ready, Bert thought, polishing off the head of his third field mouse. Each one was delicious: crunchy at first, then chewy and succulent. And then the most delicious part: the rush that came over him, the sensation of his brain exploding with thoughts and memories and connections, and the feeling that he could do anything. He ran through the moonlit woods, his paws hardly touching the ground. He jumped over rocks and fallen trees with little effort. When he finally arrived at his destination, he was barely panting, and it seemed as if only a few moments had gone by.

He was in the field with all the stones in it now, where the humans came, usually dressed in dark colors. The stones had words on them that he could now read; the humans put flowers on the stones, sometimes with tears in their eyes. Someday, he would understand all of their ways. He wasn't sure if this was a good thing.

He preferred the woods, where there were so

many warm, living things to eat. But the field with the stones gave him a view of the Cold Place. There was a fence around the Cold Place that pulsed with energy, so he knew he couldn't climb over it. But recently he'd thought of a better way.

Mellie wouldn't like it, he was sure. But he hoped she would understand.

CHAPTER TWELVE

"Aren't you going to eat?" my dad asked. "You've got a big day ahead of you. I even made you extra bacon."

He was right. I did my best to eat my breakfast, even with the twins' sneezing.

"Could you two cover your mouths?" I said. I tried to show Emmett and Ezra how to "Dracula sneeze" into their elbows, but all they did was giggle.

"Poor kiddos," my mom said, taking both their temperatures. "Their fevers have come down since last night, but I think we need to keep them home from the Harvest Festival today."

"Does that mean . . . you're not coming to see Bert and me compete?" I said. "After all our training?"

"I'm sure one of us will be able to go," my dad said.

"I need both of you there," I insisted. "For moral support."

"Maybe I can see if Mrs. Witt can watch the boys," my mom said, dialing her phone.

While my mom talked to Mrs. Witt, I finished what was on my plate, even though my stomach felt like one big knot. Bert and I just couldn't lose today—the weirdos of the world were depending on us.

My mom hung up the phone. "She said she'd be happy to watch the boys. She'll be here in an hour."

"May I be excused?" I asked.

"You may," my father said.

I scraped the crumbs off my plate and put it in the sink. "I'm going to check on Bert," I announced.

He was still curled up in his favorite spot at the foot of my bed. "It's good that you're sleeping," I said, running a hand over his newly grown-in fur. "You're going to need a lot of energy today. And a lot of focus. We both are."

Then I had a thought.

"I just realized I haven't thought about what I'm going to wear today," I said. "I need to make a good impression on the judges."

I wished I could be like Bert and have fur all over my body so I'd never have to worry about clothes. I tried on everything in my closet and nothing seemed to cut it, not even my favorite coveralls.

"Knock-knock," a voice said. "Your mom said you'd be up here."

I realized it was Mrs. Witt. "Come in," I said.

"I just wanted to wish you good luck in the contest," Mrs. Witt said, surveying my room. "I like your Marie Curie poster."

"Thanks," I said. "She's one of my heroes."

"'I was taught that the way of progress was neither swift nor easy,'" Mrs. Witt said, reading the quote on the poster. "Madame Curie wasn't kidding."

"Tell me about it," I said.

"Is this the star of today's show?" she asked, tiptoeing up to Bert. "Looks like he's sleeping pretty soundly."

"Yep. He has a big day ahead of him," I said.

"You both do," Mrs. Witt said. "Uh, it looks like . . . your closet exploded."

"I'm trying to find something to wear. You know, to impress the judges," I said.

"I might be able to help you with that," Mrs. Witt said. She held out a shopping bag.

I took it from her and opened it. Inside were Mr. Witt's lab coat and goggles.

"For me?" I said. "Really? I thought you were going to give these to your son."

"Wally is a businessman now; he doesn't have a head for chemistry, or anything sentimental," Mrs. Witt said. "I want you to have them, to thank you for all your help in Walter's workshop. I think he would like knowing they've gone to someone who loves science as much as he did."

As she handed me the coat and goggles, I thought about how glad I was that I'd done all that work for Mrs. Witt, even if it was messy and dirty and cobwebby. If I hadn't gotten to know her, I'd still be like the other kids in the neighborhood who called

her the Candy Witch. I could have missed out on knowing an interesting person.

I put the coat on. "It's a little big for me, but I think I can still wear it," I said.

Mrs. Witt smiled, but there were tears in her eyes.

"Don't worry," she said. "You'll grow into it."

CHAPTER THIRTEEN

He was dreaming of his mother.

He couldn't see her face in the dream, but he could feel her warmth curled against him, her tongue washing over his fur. He could smell her, milky and sweet.

He was purring, extending his forelegs and kneading his paws into her. He felt safe, and warm, and loved.

"Don't go," he told her, when he felt her pulling away. "Don't ever go. I need you."

"You don't need me anymore," she said. "You're not a kitten."

"Sometimes I think I am. Sometimes I'm afraid," he confessed.

"Being afraid is part of being alive. But still, we keep going," his mother said, her voice growing fainter. "You're already on your way."

"Bert?" another voice said. It sounded familiar.

He opened his eyes. Mellie was standing over him, her hand stroking his fur. She was dressed like the people in the Cold Place, with something long and white over her body, and something over her eyes shaped like another set of eyes. He growled.

"What? You don't like my lab coat? Or is it my goggles?" she asked.

Lab coat. Goggles. He felt the words click in his brain.

The girl pushed the goggles up, so they rested on top of her head.

"It's our big day," she said. "Are you ready?"

He stood up on his hind legs. "I understand you!" he shouted.

How he wished the words in his head translated. But all that came out was "Mrow! Mrow-ow!"

"I'll take that as a yes," Mellie said, scratching him behind his good ear. "Relax, Bert. Let's save our energy for the contest."

CHAPTER FOURTEEN

W hoa. It's like one big advertisement for YummCo," Danny said.

He wasn't wrong. Everything in the Green, the town square, was green and brown and plastered with the YummCo logo. The YummCo jingle was blaring from the sound system.

YummCo brings the fun-co!
The fun has just begun-co!
Be smart, not dumb-dumb-dumb-co!
And fill your day with YummCo!

There were games and rides and food stands everywhere, offering every kind of food you could imagine—and best of all, it was all free. For that reason alone, it looked like just about everyone in the town was there.

"I can't believe YummCo is paying for all this," I said. "This is generous, even for them."

"My mom and I watched an interview with Stuart Yumm this morning," Danny said. "He said the Harvest Festival is YummCo's way of giving something special to the town."

"Care for a YummCo Yummy Pizza Pouch?" one of the workers asked us. Standing behind the counter of her food stand, she held out a tray. She was smiling like she was offering us a million dollars.

"Sure," Danny said, reaching for one. But I swatted his hand away.

"Sorry," I told the worker. "We're busy."

She frowned for a moment, then quickly regained her smile and focused on the next group of people. Danny was still frowning.

"What did you do that for?" he asked. "Those pizza pouches looked pretty good."

"We're supposed to be working, not *eating*," I said. "I thought we agreed we'd both have big breakfasts so we wouldn't need to stop and eat."

"Okay, okay," Danny said. "What do you need me to do?"

"Help me find a quiet place where Bert and I can do some last-minute practicing," I said.

After a bit of walking around, we found a spot away from the crowds. I took Bert out of his carrier and snapped a leash on him, another expense that I had to take out of my savings. Immediately, Bert started to growl.

"I don't like it, either, but all animals are supposed to be leashed or caged at the festival," I said. I looked him in the eye. "Now, let's do this."

I went through the three tricks with him. First, touching the YummCo sticker on my hand. Then jumping over the toy YummCo truck. Then opening the drawer and pulling out the YummCo keychain.

Click. Gnaw. *Click*. Gnaw. *Click*. Gnaw.

"Wow," Danny said from behind his camera. "That was pretty much perfect."

"It was," I said. I let Bert chew on Mr. Peepers's head for an extra few moments as I scratched him behind his good ear. "I think we're actually going to win this."

"You're going to win what?" a familiar voice said. It was Carl. He was holding a plate of pigs in blankets from the Yummy Widdle Piggies stand. And he was wearing a suit with a green-and-brown striped tie, just like Stuart Yumm.

"Mind your own business, Carl," I said.

"Maybe next year they'll have an *Ugliest* Pet Contest," he said. "Then you'd have a chance."

"Speaking of ugly, where are your rats?" Danny asked.

Carl patted the front pocket of his suit jacket, and a tiny rat head popped out. "Zoomer's with me. My dad has Chunk, Rizzo, and Ratatouille," he explained. Just as he was about to bite into one of his Widdle Piggies, his mom appeared and snatched the plate away.

"I told you, honey, no eating on the day of a

performance," Mrs. Weems said. "I learned that in community theater. And the *Lambert Gazette* said I was the best Blanche DuBois they'd seen in at least a decade."

"But I'm not performing, my rats are!" Carl tried to explain.

"You'll be on display, too," she said. "Besides, I don't want you ruining your outfit. It took me forever to get that tailoring just right."

"Awwww," Carl moaned as Mrs. Weems popped one of the Widdle Piggies into her mouth.

"Break a leg, honey," she said, before walking away with the plate.

"What's up?" Nina Chen said as she and Owen Brown joined us. They were both in our fourth-grade class, too.

"I'm starving and my mom won't let me eat anything until after the contest," Carl grumbled. "*That's* what's up."

"Bummer," said Owen. Something rustled in the birdcage he was holding; I couldn't see what because there was a blanket over the whole thing.

"Squawk!"

"It's okay, Mudge," Owen said, patting the birdcage.

"At least you could eat this food if your mom let you," Nina said to Carl. "I have allergies, so my dad brought snacks for me. And by snacks I mean carrot and celery sticks. Blech."

"Is that a real cat?" Danny asked, peering into the carrier Nina was holding.

"This is Felicity," she said.

"She's beautiful," Danny said.

I had to admit, he was right. Felicity was all white, with long, silky fur and big blue eyes. Even Bert seemed mesmerized.

"Does she do any tricks?" Carl asked.

"Does she really have to?" Danny said.

"Not really," Nina said. "My dad says her superpower is that she throws up a lot of hairballs because her fur is so long and thick. Which reminds me, I really should go and brush her."

"I need to get Mudge his cuttlebone," said Owen. He walked off, lugging the birdcage, the bird still rustling and squawking inside.

"I should go and check on Chunk and Rizzo and Ratatouille," Carl said. "See you later, *losers*."

"Ugh," I said when Nina and Carl and Owen were all out of earshot.

"What?" said Danny.

"Nina's cat is so beautiful, it could win just by sitting there," I said. "And Carl has *four* rats. And who knows what Mudge can do?"

"Yeah, but you have Bert," Danny reminded me.

"You're always talking about how special he is. You two know these tricks forward and backward. In my opinion, there's no competition."

"Okay," I said.

Danny took me by the shoulders and looked right at me.

"Repeat after me: *There is no competition*," he said.

"*There is no competition*," I said.

"Mrow, mrow-ow," said Bert.

"Sometimes I feel like you really understand me," I told Bert.

He blinked at me. I blinked back.

"I think we're ready," I said.

CHAPTER FIFTEEN

I'm glad you don't have to work at the festival today," Roxanne Hurley said, squeezing Greg's arm.

"Me too," said Greg. He felt guilty knowing that just hanging out with Roxanne was his work. He tried to make up for it: he won a big YummCo teddy bear at the ring toss, and he got her a YummCo Slusher and a plate of YummCo Super Cheezy Nachos, both in size HUGE. They may have been free, but that didn't make them easier to carry.

"Do you want to try these nachos, honey?" she asked.

"They do look delicious," he said. But just as he was about to grab a Super Cheezy chip, someone pulled on his other arm. It was Kari. She was wearing a headset and wielding her YummPad like she meant business, though Greg couldn't think of a time when Kari *didn't* mean business.

"Hey," she said. "I need to talk to you."

"Is this one of your colleagues from work, Greg?" Roxanne asked.

"This is Kari," Greg explained.

"Kari?" Roxanne repeated. She raised her eyebrows. "I'm Roxanne. Greg has told me so much about you."

"I hope not," Kari said, ignoring Roxanne's outstretched hand. She looked at Greg. "We need to talk. Now."

"Looks like something has come up," Greg said to Roxanne. "Save some nachos for me?"

"Of course," she said.

"So, what's wrong?" he asked Kari when they were finally alone.

"What *isn't* wrong?" she said. "I mean, look at everyone, enjoying all the free games and rides and gorging themselves on all this free food. You have no idea how much money we're wasting on all this."

"But this Harvest Festival isn't about making a profit," Greg reminded her. "The Big Boss said that it's about getting Y-91 back *and* giving something special to Lambert. I actually think it's sweet."

"Sweet?" Kari repeated, narrowing her eyes. "That's the *last* word I'd use to describe the Big Boss."

Just then, the YummCo jingle stopped playing over the sound system. A high-pitched squeal filled the air as someone turned on the microphone at the main stage.

"Ladies and gentlemen, boys and girls," a voice said. "Are you ready to find out who the Best Pet in Lambert is?"

The crowd cheered, wearing their YummCo baseball hats, waving their YummCo pennants, the children holding their green and brown balloons, drinking their slushers, and eating their nachos and pizza pouches and pigs in blankets and corn dogs.

"Look, everyone's having a blast," Greg said. "Try to enjoy yourself, too. You put a lot of work into this day."

Kari almost smiled. Greg was the only one who noticed her efforts—why did he have to be so *nice*? Somehow that made him even more annoying.

She adjusted her headset and told the stage manager to double-check the microphone levels. Then she glared at Greg.

"We're not here to enjoy ourselves. We have a job to do," Kari reminded him. "Come on. The big event's about to start."

CHAPTER SIXTEEN

Hello, Lambert! Are you ready to bring the *fun-co?*" Mr. Yumm yelled. I grimaced at the screech of feedback from the microphone. Nina covered her ears. The rest of the crowd went wild.

"YummCo! YummCo! YummCo!" they chanted. A little boy on his father's shoulders waved a big green foam thumbs-up. Mr. Yumm noticed it in the crowd and gave everyone a real thumbs-up, his trademark. The crowd went even wilder.

"I want to introduce you to the most beautiful little lady in the YummCo family, the one who brings the joy and the fun-co to my life every day," the CEO said, extending an arm to the other side of the stage.

Out walked Mr. Yumm's daughter, Yolanda. In her arms was a tiny, fluffy brown dog wearing a green-and-brown striped collar.

"Arf-arf!" the dog yapped.

"Oh, did you think I was talking about my daughter?" Mr. Yumm said, grinning as he kissed Yolanda on the cheek and took the dog from her. "Yolanda is just great, as you all know. But of course, I meant the newest addition to the YummCo family—my dog, Yummikins!"

"Aw, isn't it cute?" Nina said from where we were all standing offstage.

"It looks like a shih-poo," Carl said.

"It sure does," said Danny, holding his nose.

"A shih-poo is a cross between a shih tzu and a toy poodle," Carl said. "My parents were going to get me a dog before I found my rats at YummCo Animal Pals."

"You chose *rats* over a *dog?*" Danny said. "I'd love to have a dog, but our landlord doesn't allow any pets."

"Wait, doesn't YummCo own your building?" I asked.

"Exactly," Danny said, rolling his eyes.

"Rats are smart," Carl reminded us. "Plus, you don't have to get up every morning to walk them."

He had a point. But I was too busy watching Yolanda. She was so amazing, helping her dad run YummCo *and* running her lifestyle blog, *Yumm Life*. Not to mention she somehow managed to get her hair so shiny and perfectly styled.

Yolanda leaned into the microphone. "Oh, *Dad*!" she said, rolling her eyes playfully and laughing. Even her teeth were perfect.

"It's time we started the big contest," Mr. Yumm said. "I'd give the award to Yummikins, but I'm told that would be nepotism!"

Everyone in the crowd started laughing.

"What's nepotism?" Nina asked.

"It's when you give a job to someone just because they're family," Danny explained.

"Kinda like Mr. Yumm letting Yolanda help him run YummCo?" asked Owen.

"Yolanda is more than qualified," I said. "She went to YummCo University, after all."

"Let's get the first contestant up here," Mr. Yumm

announced. Yolanda handed him a clipboard. "Looks like that would be Owen Brown and his pet budgie, Mudge!"

"Here goes nothing," Owen said, taking a deep breath.

He brought the birdcage out onto the stage and removed the blanket over it. Inside was a small blue bird. The bird shifted from one end of its perch to the other and cocked its head.

"What would you like to say to Mr. Yumm, Mudge?" Owen asked.

"YummCo brings the fun-co!" the bird squawked. "YummCo brings the fun-co!"

"Wow. A *talking* pet?" Danny said. He looked at me. "Forget what I said before. You do have competition."

"Thanks a *lot*," I said. "I already knew that—I just didn't know how much."

After the applause finally died down, Nina and Felicity went next. Nina stood with her legs about a foot apart, and Felicity darted in and out between them. Then she rolled on the floor and played dead when Nina pointed at her. The crowd oohed and aahed.

An elderly couple went next, with their pair of Yorkies, Sven and Gwen, who were supposed to jump through hoops. Gwen made a pretty good effort, but Sven seemed more interested in licking himself.

And then it was Carl's turn. The crowd just about gave him a standing ovation for the suit his mom made for him. Mr. Yumm seemed particularly impressed.

"Looks like our lab's cloning experiment was a success," Mr. Yumm said, wiggling his eyebrows. Everyone in the crowd laughed.

Carl took a little silver whistle out of his jacket pocket. He opened the cage at one end of the stage and stood at the other end. When he blew into the whistle, no sound seemed to come out. But all four of his rats scampered across the stage toward him and leaped onto his shoulders.

"Do you think it's a dog whistle?" Danny asked. I shrugged.

One by one, the rats performed different tricks. They played fetch. They jumped through hoops. They took turns shaking Carl's hand. And then they all

faced the audience and waved. If Bert and I weren't competing against them, I'd be pretty impressed. Instead, I was panicking. How were we ever going to win now?

Bert must have been thinking the same thing because he started pulling against the leash. I scratched him behind his good ear.

"Everything's okay," I told him. "Don't worry, stage fright is totally normal."

"Finally, we have Mellie Gore and her cat, Bert!" Mr. Yumm read off the clipboard.

"Go win one for the weirdos," Danny said, clapping me on the shoulder.

I was ready, but Bert still seemed nervous. He wouldn't let me lead him up the stairs by his leash, so I ended up having to carry him.

"It's okay," I whispered. "We've got this."

"What an . . . interesting-looking animal," Yolanda said when we got to the stage. She leaned down to pet Bert.

"That's probably not a good idea. He's . . . a little nervous," I said.

"Well, what sort of *fun-co* are you two going to bring to us today?" Mr. Yumm asked.

"Bert is going to do some tricks," I said.

I was about to set up the toy YummCo truck and the jewelry box on the stage when Bert looked up at the Yumms, then out at the audience. Then he puffed up his fur until he was about twice his normal size and started hissing.

"Impressive," said Mr. Yumm. He made notes on his clipboard. Yolanda did, too.

"That's not the—" I started to say, but then Bert started growling and straining at his leash harder than ever. Over in the wings, I saw Felicity jump into Nina's arms. Everyone in the crowd seemed to take a

step back. Even Yummikins looked a little bit freaked out.

"Come on, Bert," I said. I put the YummCo sticker on my hand and held it out. "Everything's going to be fine."

And that's when he went totally crazy. He growled louder than I'd ever heard before, then leaped into the air and spun around like he was looking for a way to escape. I was still holding on to the leash, so he ended up landing on me, his front claws digging into my arm.

"Whoa!" I cried.

"Now *that* was a performance," Mr. Yumm said into the microphone. "And Halloween isn't until next week!"

"Let's hear it for Mellie and Bert, and all our wonderful contestants!" Yolanda added.

"But we didn't even . . ." I tried to explain, but Yolanda didn't hear me. She was too focused on the crowd.

"We'll announce the winner in just a few moments!" she said.

Then she started clapping, and the crowd followed suit. I took that as our cue to leave the stage, and so did Bert—he just about pulled me down the stairs and over to where Danny was standing.

"What was *that?*" he asked.

"I . . . I don't know," I said. The whole thing had left me in a daze. I looked down at Bert and rubbed my arm where he'd scratched me. "He just . . . wasn't himself up there."

"You can say that again," Danny said. "He looks better now, though."

By this time, Bert had deflated back to normal. You'd never know he'd nearly attacked everyone onstage. I reached out my hand to touch him, and I could feel his heart beating a mile a minute.

"Are you okay?" I asked him.

CHAPTER SEVENTEEN

He thought he would be braver when he finally saw his nemesis. He remembered what his mother had said in his dream, that he should keep going. But his fear got the better of him.

He felt bad for Mellie, who'd expected him to perform. And he'd never wanted to hurt her. But he didn't expect all the people waving and shouting, the harsh lights, and the One, right there next to him.

He remembered his time back at the Cold Place, the tests that made his eyes burn and his skin itch and his stomach tie up in knots. The tests that made him weak, so weak. The tests that took his sister away, then his brother. The Rough Hands, holding him down on the cold table. And the One, directing their cruel efforts.

It was as if he had no control over himself when he was up there onstage. His mind had gone back to the Cold Place, and his body took over. He felt himself expand, his claws extend, a cry—of fear, of sadness, of anger—explode from his deepest self. And once it was over, he heard Mellie cry out, and then he saw her face. It was she who seemed afraid.

Never again, he vowed, closing his eyes and willing his heart to beat more slowly. *From now on, I must be in control.*

CHAPTER EIGHTEEN

We brought you a Yumm Dog, Mellie," Mom said, holding out a corn dog on a green stick.

"No thanks," I said. Even if I weren't so upset, it still wouldn't look appetizing.

My mom took a bite. "It's not bad, actually," she said, offering it to my dad, who took a bite, too.

"Mmm, tasty," he said, swallowing. "We should *definitely* post a video about all this Harvest Festival food. YummCo would love that!" Then he turned to me. "You should feel good about this, sweetheart. You worked really hard—animals are just unpredictable."

I wanted to believe my dad. Bert could be unpredictable. But there was something about the way he was acting that felt *really* off. It reminded me of the time Danny and I tried to take Bert to YummCo Animal Pals; we were hoping to get him a checkup, but he'd freaked out before we'd even walked through the door. I remember Danny was super disappointed because the Yumms were there that day and he'd wanted to get a selfie with Mr. Yumm.

"Think of it this way," Danny said, snapping me out of my memory. "You were probably going to lose to Nina and Felicity or Owen and Mudge or Chuck and his rats anyway. Or even that couple with Sven and Gwen. Gwen had potential."

"Why doesn't that make me feel better?" I said. I rubbed my arm and looked down at Bert, who was curled up on the grass, his eyes closed.

Yolanda Yumm's voice came over the loudspeaker.

"Ladies and gentlemen, we've just tallied our votes, and we're pleased to announce the winner of the first annual YummCo Best Pet Contest!"

"Great," I said, putting my head in my hands.

"Ugh, the suspense is *killing* me," my mom said.

She took another bite of corn dog, then passed it back to my dad.

"Everyone put your hands together for . . . Mellie Gore and her cat, Bert!"

"What?" I said, looking up. Danny's jaw dropped. My dad had just taken another bite of corn dog; he gulped loudly.

"Maybe we heard it wrong," Danny said, staring at the loudspeaker.

"We couldn't have *all* heard it wrong," Dad said.

"Honey," my mom said, putting her hand on my back. "I think . . . you won?"

"Mellie? Bert? Are you out there?" Yolanda called. "Come on up and get your big prize!"

Somehow, I managed to get Bert back to the stage, though it seemed to take forever since he was hissing and straining at the leash again. When we got there, Yolanda handed me the check for two hundred dollars, and one of the YummCo employees struggled to put a brand-new YummCo collar on Bert. She was wearing special gloves to handle him, like the ones they had at the vet's.

"Be careful," I said. "He really doesn't like being onstage."

Finally, the assistant managed to clip the collar on him. "Really? He seems fine to me," she said. She was right; Bert seemed super calm, though his eyes were wider than ever.

A photographer ran up and aimed a camera at us. I could see my parents offstage, filming it all. I couldn't believe it; Bert and I actually did it. Score one for the weirdos. But it didn't really feel like a win; we didn't perform well at all compared to all the other acts. What exactly did the Yumms see in us?

"Congratulations," Yolanda said into the microphone, shaking my hand. I smiled just as the camera's flash went off. I had a feeling my eyes were closed for the actual photo.

I stood on tiptoe to reach the mic. "Thank you," I said.

"And how does Bert feel about being the Best Pet in Lambert?" she asked. We both looked down at him. He just stared out into space, and he looked stiff, almost like he was frozen.

"Uh," I said. "I think we're both really shocked."

"Well, he's going to be really *excited* to ride in the Harvest Festival parade on the YummCo float with us!" she said. "Everyone, let's give a hand to our big winners!"

The audience started clapping again. My mom shouted, "Go, Mellie!" and my dad put his fingers in his mouth and whistled. None of this seemed real. The more I thought about it, the weirder it seemed.

I followed Yolanda and the YummCo employee she called Kari. But Kari turned around and stopped me.

"Sorry," she said. "We don't have room for you on the float."

"But I thought the winner was supposed to ride with the Yumms," I said.

"Right," she said. "The winning *pet*." She seemed distracted by whoever was talking to her on her headset.

"He really should stay with me. He hasn't been himself all day," I said as she took Bert from me. He seemed very still and he didn't make a sound, but his eyes were wider than ever.

"Don't worry. I've been around animals a lot," Kari said. "We'll take it from here."

"No, really. I should be with him. He isn't feeling—" I tried to explain, but Kari was already talking into her headset.

"Everything's a go," she said. Then she barely looked at me and said, "You can meet us at the end of the parade route."

"Okay," I said. But it didn't feel okay. As Kari carried Bert down to the float and put him in Mr. Yumm's waiting arms, Bert seemed so small and lost. I wanted to say something more to him, to let him know he was safe. But by then the float had already taken off, with the Yumms waving to the crowd.

That's when it hit me. Bert freaked out at YummCo Animal Pals, and he was freaking out now. Both times, the Yumms were there.

Was Bert afraid of the Yumms?

CHAPTER NINETEEN

Once they put the collar on, he couldn't move, and he couldn't think.

The lights and sounds around him were muffled, as if there were something surrounding him—a tight, invisible blanket, preventing him from escaping or crying out. The Rough Hands had already found a way to place him under their control.

He wanted to say something to Mellie. She was watching them take him away, and there was fear in her eyes. He wanted to tell her not to be afraid, but he was too busy telling himself, *Being afraid is part of being alive. But still, we keep going.*

He had no choice now. He was in the clutches of the One, and there was no turning back.

CHAPTER TWENTY

I tried to follow the whole parade route, but there were just too many people lining Main Street. Every now and then I got a glimpse of the big green-and-brown float cruising by, with the Yumms waving and throwing YummCo candy to the kids. The marching band ahead of them played a brassy version of the YummCo jingle, and everyone in the crowd seemed to be singing along.

YummCo brings the fun-co!

The fun has just begun-co!

Be smart, not dumb-dumb-dumb-co!

And fill your day with YummCo!

Close to the end of the route, I spotted Danny, standing on a park bench. He was filming.

"Why aren't you down there?" he said, aiming his phone at the float.

"They said there wasn't enough room," I said. "Something *really* weird is going on. I think it has to do with the Yumms."

"Everything looks normal from here," Danny said. "Though it looks like there would have been plenty of room on the float for you."

"Can you see Bert?" I asked.

"Yep, he's front and center, right in the big man's arms," Danny said. "I'm surprised he's so calm. Bert, I mean."

He handed me his phone so I could look through it. There Bert was, in Mr. Yumm's arms. He looked like he was almost asleep.

I gave Danny his phone. "I'm going to run

down there and meet up with Bert," I said. "Are you coming?"

"Are you kidding? This is the perfect position for filming," Danny said. "Honestly, you'll get a better view up here with me."

I sighed. Danny was Danny, and that was that.

When I got to the end of the parade route, I had to push through all the marching band members carrying their instruments. I almost collided with a tuba player when I saw the big green-and-brown YummCo limousine. The driver had just closed the door.

"I'm so sorry," Kari said, stepping in front of me. Even though she wasn't much bigger than me, I couldn't get around her.

"Where's Bert?" I asked.

"Your cat had another episode up on the float. It nearly bit Mr. Yumm, and then it ran away," she explained.

"*What?* How could you let that happen?" I cried.

"We didn't *let* it happen. That animal is clearly disturbed," Kari said.

I looked all around the busy festival. *Bert really is afraid of the Yumms*, I thought. *But why?*

"Do you at least know what direction he ran?" I asked.

"It all happened so fast. Honestly, I couldn't tell you," Kari said. She said something I couldn't hear into her headset, then turned and got into the limo.

"Bert!" I called. "Bert, where are you?"

"Mellie!" my mom shouted. She ran toward me, my dad close behind, holding a mint chocolate chip YummCo Yummy Cone. "Where have you been?"

"We looked for you on the YummCo float," Dad said, licking the cone to keep up with the melting ice cream.

"I don't have time to explain," I said. "Bert is lost."

"That cat has always gone his own way," Mom said. "Just like you."

"You don't understand. Something is *really* wrong," I tried to explain.

"I'm sure Bert will show up at home eventually, like he always does," my dad said.

I looked at them both. They seemed tired. I remembered how they'd both been up with Emmett and Ezra the night before, nursing their colds. Maybe it hadn't been such a good idea to make them come out today.

"I'm going to look around for him a little bit more here," I said. "I'll see you at home."

"Good luck," Mom said.

"I'm sure he'll turn up, honey," my dad added.

After they left, I did my best to keep searching, but there were just too many people around for me to see anything. Where could he have gone? I was just about to go home and look for Bert there when Danny came running toward me.

"You aren't going to believe this," he said. I wasn't in the mood to hear about his dramatic shots and perfect film angles. And I definitely wasn't in the mood for Owen and Nina and Carl, who showed up, too.

"Hey, we've been looking for you everywhere," Nina said. "We didn't have a chance to congratulate you."

"It was pretty unbelievable that Bert won," Owen said.

"Yeah," Carl said, his eyes narrow. "Unbelievable. As in *not believable at all*."

"Where is Bert anyway?" Nina asked.

"He's gone, and I can't find him anywhere," I said, fighting back tears. "He had another meltdown and jumped off the float and ran away."

"I don't think that's true," Danny said. He handed me his phone. "You need to watch this."

I wiped my eyes and hit play.

"You're right, you did have the perfect position for filming," I said. His footage of the parade was pretty great, particularly the YummCo float. I could see just about every one of Yolanda's perfect teeth and the brown-and-green stripes on Mr. Yumm's tie. And I could see Bert, his eyes wide, in Mr. Yumm's arms. He looked so afraid.

"Keep watching," Danny said.

"I don't know if I want to see his meltdown," I said, wincing. But when the float finally reached the end of the parade route, Bert hadn't moved. He almost seemed like a statue of himself. And then I saw it.

Kari picked up Bert and put him in a waiting cat carrier. Then she placed the cat carrier in the back of the Yumms' limousine!

I blinked. I looked up at Danny.

"I couldn't believe it, either," he said.

"So Bert had a good reason to be afraid of the Yumms," I said.

"I *knew* that contest was rigged," Carl said.

"Kari *lied* to me," I said.

"But why?" Danny asked.

"And why would the Yumms want your cat?" asked Nina.

"There's something rotten at YummCo, and I'm going to find out what it is," I said.

"Let's go get our bikes," Danny said. He turned to the others. "Are you coming, too?"

Carl hesitated. "You want us to help?" he said.

"You all know you'd want everyone to help if something happened to one of your pets," Danny said. Then he looked at Carl. "Remember how worried Mellie was when you thought something happened to Chunk a few weeks ago?"

"You did come by to check on her, which was nice," Carl admitted, giving me a nod.

"I don't know what I'd do if something happened

to Felicity," Nina said, looking down at her cat carrier. Inside, Felicity yawned.

"Or Mudge," said Owen.

"Squawk! YummCo brings the fun-co!" Mudge said from his cage.

"I guess it's settled, then," I said. "Let's do this."

CHAPTER TWENTY-ONE

Y ummikins, calm down," Stuart Yumm said to his beloved shih-poo. But the dog only growled louder and bared her fangs at the cat carrier on the floor of the limo. The cat inside stared back with wide yellow eyes.

"You really should put this back on it," Yolanda said, handing her father the green-and-brown collar the dog was wearing before. "That animal is out of control."

"She's merely spirited," Mr. Yumm said. But once he put the collar on Yummikins, the dog calmed down immediately.

"You need to show it *you're* the boss," Yolanda said.

"And what would you know about that, sweetheart?" her father said, chuckling. He knocked on the glass partition between the back seat and the driver. "Can this thing go any faster?"

"It could. But then we'd be breaking the law, sir," the driver said.

"I *am* the law around here," Mr. Yumm informed him.

"Sir, we don't want to risk getting into an accident," Kari said, motioning to the cat carrier. "Not when we're transporting such precious cargo."

"I don't understand why I couldn't stay at the parade with Roxanne," Greg said, looking out the window. "It's not like you really need me here."

"Because you're not supposed to be with *them*. You're with *us*," Kari reminded him.

"Yeah, well, it looks like *they* are about to be with *us* fairly soon," Greg said. He pointed out the back window. "Look."

Behind them, five figures on bicycles were following the limo. They seemed to be gaining on them.

Kari pounded on the partition glass.

"You heard Mr. Yumm," she shouted at the driver. "STEP ON IT!"

"And do whatever it takes to lose those kids," Yolanda added.

CHAPTER TWENTY-TWO

T he limo's speeding up!" I shouted at Danny. "We're going to lose them!"

"Well, we know where they're going—either the YummCo campus or the mansion!" Danny shouted back.

"We'll go to the campus," Carl said, signaling for Nina and Owen to follow him.

"Do any of you have a phone?" Danny asked.

"I do," Nina said. They exchanged numbers.

"If you find anything, let us know. We'll do the same," Danny said. Nina nodded, and they pedaled off.

Danny and I followed the limo, which made a sharp right just before the middle school.

"They're taking a shortcut through the cemetery," I said.

"I know that place like the back of my hand," Danny said. I believed him; it was one of his favorite filming locations. I let him lead us away from the limo and down some side paths meant for walking. Thankfully there weren't any funerals there that day or we would have had a serious problem.

"If we make it quick, we can head them off," said Danny. "Pedal faster."

"I'm trying!" I said. But I was also wondering what we were going to do if we managed to stop the limo. And I was also thinking about Bert. Was he okay? Was he scared? What did the Yumms want with him? I knew it didn't feel right when Kari told me I couldn't ride on the float with him, and when he seemed so freaked out. I should never have let her take him.

Twisting and turning around the headstones and monuments, we finally made it to the other side of the cemetery. And just in the nick of time, too. The limo was coming right for us.

"Are they going to hit us?" I shouted.

"They wouldn't," Danny said.

RRRRRRRRRTTTTTTT! The brakes squealed. I winced, bracing for impact.

But the limo stopped short, just about a foot before Danny's front bike wheel. Immediately, he took out his phone and started dialing. I took out my phone and started taking photos. At the same time, Kari got out of the limo and stormed toward us.

"What are you doing? Get out of the way!" she shouted. "And stop taking pictures!"

She tried to grab my phone, but I pulled it away.

"Why? We're not on YummCo property," I said. I snapped a couple of extra photos of her for good measure.

It was then that someone else got out of the limo.

"Greg?" I said.

"What?" he said, shrugging. "You knew I worked at YummCo."

"I didn't know you worked for *them*," I said.

Danny put his hand over his phone. "You used us," he said. "You used my mom."

"I liked your mom. A lot. I still do, actually," Greg said. "Can you let her know? Are you on the phone with her now?"

"I'm on the phone with the *police* now. They'll be here any minute," Danny informed him.

"What is the meaning of this?" Mr. Yumm said, poking his head out.

"Dad, just stay in the car," I could hear Yolanda tell him from inside the limo. "This will all be over soon."

"Yeah, it will," I said. "For you."

The sound of a siren cut through the air, and a police cruiser soon pulled up beside the limo. An officer got out and took a few steps toward all of us, clearly assessing the situation.

I looked at Mr. Yumm and Greg and Kari and smirked. But not for long.

"Good afternoon, Mr. Yumm," the officer said.

"Well, hello there, Dave," Mr. Yumm said, grinning. "How are the wife and kids?"

"Just great," said the officer. "Thanks so much for the gift baskets you sent to me and the other officers."

"It's the least YummCo can do for our boys in blue," Mr. Yumm said. "Though I'm thinking brand-new green-and-brown uniforms and police cruisers might be in order."

"That sounds swell, sir," said Officer Dave. "Now what seems to be the trouble?"

"These children are blocking our path," Yolanda called from inside the limo.

"You'll need to move out of the way," Officer Dave said to me and Danny.

"Wait a minute," Danny said. "*I* was the one who called you. These people have stolen my friend's cat."

"Your *what*, now?" Officer Dave asked.

"My cat, Bert," I said. I pointed to the limo. "He's right there inside."

Kari flipped open her YummPad. "I don't know what this *child* is talking about, officer. This feral cat found its way onto the YummCo premises and was exposed to some hazardous materials. It escaped from our lab several weeks ago while it was under observation."

"*Unintentionally* exposed to hazardous materials," Stuart Yumm added. "Because, of course, we maintain our pledge not to experiment on animals."

I remembered Danny and I had seen a hazmat team searching the town one night a few weeks ago. Two of them had even chased us in their van. Was it Bert they'd been after all along? It couldn't be true.

"But he's *mine*," I pleaded.

"This particular animal is the property of YummCo. You'll note that all of the paperwork is in order," Kari said. "We'll be taking it back to the lab for further observation."

Now she was the one who was smirking. Greg was shrugging, like he was still trying to convince us that none of this was his fault. Mr. Yumm had his arms crossed and his face was red. Yolanda was still in the limo; clearly, I wasn't even worth worrying about.

And Bert was in there, too. It hurt my heart that I couldn't see him, even just to know he was okay.

"No," I cried, hanging my head.

"You two'd best get out of the way and get home before I have to have a talk with your parents," Officer Dave told me and Danny. He looked at Mr. Yumm. "So sorry you had to deal with this trouble, sir."

"You've dealt with it for me," Mr. Yumm said. He uncrossed his arms and gave Dave his signature thumbs-up.

Dave gave him a thumbs-up in return. "You have a nice day, now," he said to Mr. Yumm and Greg and Kari. He stood there until they all got back into the limo and drove off toward the Yumms' mansion.

"What do we do now?" Danny whispered. I shook my head; I didn't have a plan B. Unless you counted this plan, which was B for busted. I dug my hands into my lab coat pockets. And that's when I felt . . . something. It was a slip of paper with a bit of writing on it. I knew from all the organizing I'd done in Mr. Witt's workshop that the handwriting was his.

Open the gift that keeps on giving, it said. That was what the plaque said on the big framed photo Mr.

Witt had in his workshop. The photo of the Witts Confectionery grand opening. It was probably some kind of anniversary reminder, I figured.

"Run along, kids," said Officer Dave. "I'm going to let you go with a warning this time. But if I see you making trouble for the Yumms again, that's going to be trouble for you two. Got it?"

"Got it," Danny said. I was still looking down at the slip of paper when he nudged me.

"Yes, sir," I added, shoving the note back in my pocket.

We got on our bikes and started pedaling, and Officer Dave followed us home.

The whole time, I didn't say a word to Danny. I didn't even look at him. I was feeling sad and hopeless before. Now I was feeling something else.

"Let's go to my house," I called to Danny. And then I started pedaling faster.

CHAPTER TWENTY-THREE

*O*nce the limo arrived at Yumm Mansion, everyone went inside and got down to business. Kari and Greg brought the cat carrier into the Big Boss's study.

"Well, *that* was annoying," Kari said.

"Children often are," said the Big Boss, taking a seat behind the desk.

"At least we don't have to deal with *those* children anymore," Kari said. "We got what we wanted."

"Yes. We did," said the Big Boss, patting the cat carrier.

"That was some nice improvising with that bit about the hazardous materials," Greg said to Kari.

"I thought we should have a backup story, just in case," Kari explained. "I drew up the paperwork this morning."

"I knew you had a head for details," the Big Boss said. Kari blushed.

"Is it okay in there?" Greg asked. He peered inside. "The cat looks pretty out of it."

"It's just the clipnosis collar," Kari said.

"Clipnosis?" said Greg.

"You can render some animals immobile just by pinching the scruff of their neck. The collar is the Big Boss's invention," Kari explained. She reached in and unclipped it from Y-91.

The cat blinked and looked around. The Big Boss leaned down to the carrier and grinned.

"I've got big plans for you, Y-91. *Huge*."

CHAPTER TWENTY-FOUR

About an hour later, Danny and I were sitting at the picnic table in my backyard, and I was talking a mile a minute when Carl and Nina and Owen showed up.

"We made it to the campus," Carl said.

"We looked all around, but we couldn't find a way in," Owen explained.

"That was when we got your text," Nina said. "What happened?"

Danny and I looked at each other. We both took deep breaths and started explaining how we'd managed to stop the limo and call the police.

"The cop turned out to be friends with the Yumms, so he let them get away," Danny said.

"Because they claim Bert is some kind of biohazard. Which I'm sure is another *lie*," I added, rolling my eyes. "So the cop let them take him."

"Bummer," said Owen.

"Though you did take all those photos of them being stopped by the police," Carl reminded me. "You could send them to the *Lambert Gazette*. The last thing the Yumms would want is bad publicity on their big Harvest Festival day."

"I didn't think of that!" I said. I scrolled through the photos on my phone. And scrolled. And scrolled.

"What's wrong?" Danny asked.

"They're . . . gone," I said. I looked at Danny. "How about your video from today?"

Danny searched on his phone. "It's not there, either," he said. "Ugh. There goes our evidence and the new footage for my movie."

I looked at my phone, then at Danny's.

"Wait," I said. "We both have YummPhones. Think that's a coincidence?"

"Whoa. That's like, *cyber crime*," Owen said.

"You know what? It doesn't matter. We're not giving up that easily," I informed them.

"We're not?" Nina said.

"Nope," I said. "And now we've got them right where we want them. Because we're kids, they've underestimated us."

"Big mistake," Danny said.

"Huge," I added, doing my best Stuart Yumm impression.

Carl's stomach growled. "It's just about dinnertime. I haven't eaten all day, thanks to my mom," he said. He patted the pocket of his blazer, and a little rat head popped out. "And I've fed Zoomer just about all of his rat pellets."

"Do you bring that thing everywhere with you?" Nina asked.

"Don't tell the other rats, but he's my favorite," Carl said.

"I haven't eaten, either. All that free food, and I didn't eat a *single bite*," Danny said, glaring at me.

"What?" I said. "We agreed we wouldn't eat at the Harvest Festival so we'd have more time to practice with Bert."

"I'm hungry, too. But I don't know what we're eating tonight at my house," Owen said. "My mom started coming down with something after lunch."

"My dad's sick, too, and my brother," Nina said. "Something must be going around."

"It's probably the cold my brothers have. I think my parents are coming down with it, too," I said, remembering how tired they looked at the festival.

Danny tossed Owen his phone. "Tell your parents we're having dinner here—to celebrate Mellie's big win. We can order pizza while we figure out our plan."

"That is, if you're still with us," I said. I looked at Carl, then at Owen and Nina.

"If anyone wants out, now is the time," Danny said. "You can go home and forget about all of this."

Carl fidgeted a bit, but no one moved. Danny looked at me and smiled.

"Okay," I said, leaning forward.

Just as I was about to tell them my plan, the back door of my house swung open, and Mrs. Witt came running out.

"Mellie—something is wrong!" she said breathlessly. "With your parents!"

"I'll be right back," I told everyone. I followed Mrs. Witt inside.

My dad was standing in front of the open freezer, his face buried in a gallon of YummCo mint chocolate chip ice cream. The ice cream was dribbling down his beard and the front of his shirt.

"Dad?" I asked.

When he turned to look at me, I could see his eyes were wide and blank.

"Gaaah!" I screamed, backing up to the kitchen counter.

"When they first came home from the festival, they told me they weren't feeling well," Mrs. Witt explained. "They said they were going to lie down, so I went upstairs to check on the twins. When I came back down, this is what I found."

"Dad, what happened to you? What's wrong?"

"It's . . . so good," he said, between bites of ice cream. "*So. Good.*"

As I tried to process what was happening, I had a thought: *Emmett and Ezra.*

"Are the twins okay?" I asked Mrs. Witt. "They were sick yesterday and this morning."

"They're fine. No more fevers and no sniffles. And they don't . . . look different, like this," she said, motioning to my dad. "They're taking a nap upstairs."

"Where's my mom?" I asked Mrs. Witt. She gestured toward the dining room.

Mom was at the dining room table, her back to me. All her credit cards were fanned out in front of her, and her fingers were tapping frantically at the keyboard of her YummBook. The television in the living room was blaring.

"Mom, what are you doing?" I asked.

"There are so many things we need," she said. "*So. Many.*"

I looked over her shoulder at the laptop screen. She was on the YummCo website, ordering thousands of dollars of merchandise: camera equipment, electronics, clothes and toys for Emmett and Ezra. A laboratory-grade microscope for me. I thought about how much I wanted that microscope . . . just not this way.

"Mom, we can't afford all this stuff!" I shouted.

She whipped around to face me. Her eyes were wide and blank, and she was salivating.

"We can't affort *not* to have it!" she shouted. "I won't allow this family to go without!"

"Mom?" I said, shaking. But she didn't look like my mom anymore. She looked like an animal.

Just then, a YummCo commercial appeared on the television. It was a new one I'd never seen before. Stuart Yumm was front and center, grinning from ear to ear.

"People of Lambert, head on down to Super YummCo today!" the voiceover announcer said. "We've got something *huge* in store for you—*fresh, new* products for the whole family! You just can't *live* without them!"

Then Mr. Yumm gave his trademark thumbs-up as the YummCo jingle started playing.

YummCo brings the fun-co!

The fun has just begun-co!

Be smart, not dumb-dumb-dumb-co!

And fill your day with YummCo!

"YummCo brings the fun-co," my mom repeated in a voice that made her sound like a sleepy robot. "The fun has just begun-co."

She stood, knocking over the dining room chair. Then she grabbed her credit cards and started to walk toward the back door, her eyes wide and glassy, saliva pooling in the corners of her mouth. When she passed my dad in the kitchen, he finally stopped eating.

"Be smart, not dumb-dumb-dumb-co," he said in the same sleepy robot voice. "And fill your day with YummCo."

He dropped the ice cream and followed her. The gallon of YummCo mint chocolate chip landed on our kitchen floor with a bright green-and-brown *SPLAT*.

Mrs. Witt looked at me. We both blinked for a few seconds, taking it all in.

"I think . . . the twins should stay with you for a little while," I said finally, trying to stay calm. "And don't let them eat any YummCo products." Mrs. Witt nodded.

Danny ran into the kitchen. "You've got to come out and see this," he said.

Mrs. Witt and I followed him outside. We joined Owen and Nina and Carl in my driveway, watching all our neighbors, young and old, chanting the YummCo jingle and shambling down the street like they were sleepwalking. They were all salivating, and they had the same glassy expression as my parents. And they were all headed in the same direction. Toward Super YummCo.

"They're like . . . *real zombies*," Danny said. For the first time, he seemed too freaked out to film anything.

"We saw your mom and dad headed there, too," Owen told me.

"And we couldn't get any of our parents on the phone," Nina said.

"What is going *on?*" Carl asked.

"There's only one way to find out," I said.

"What?" asked Danny.

I pointed. "Follow that horde."

Owen and Nina started after the shambling, drooling YummCo zombies, with Carl and Danny close behind.

I looked at Mrs. Witt.

"I'll be here," she said, putting a hand on my shoulder. "Be careful."

As I followed my friends, I reached into my lab coat pocket and felt Mr. Witt's note. *Open the gift that keeps on giving.* It was just an anniversary reminder . . . or was it? Absolutely nothing made sense right now. All I could do was hope we weren't headed in the wrong direction.

"Wait for me!" I called to Danny and the others, running to catch up.

CHAPTER TWENTY-FIVE

He felt himself being carried, down stairs and dark, winding hallways. All the while, he thought of Mellie. He wished he could have said goodbye to her. He thought he'd heard her calling his name, though things had been so foggy until now.

He knew he was back in the Cold Place when he saw and heard the code being pressed on the security keypad. The heavy door opened, with its familiar *whoosh*, and then closed behind them. Immediately, the harsh smells hit his nose, including the smell of blood. Someone had tried to wash it away, but he could still smell it: the blood, and the fear.

They put him back in the lab cage marked Y-91, the Rough Hands grabbing him, pushing him in, then locking the door. The door on the cage was new, he noticed, and this time, there would be no escape from it. The other animals soon began whimpering, some even wailing, and it was as if he had never left. Almost. As he looked around, he realized all the animals were different. Where were the others, the ones he'd promised to rescue?

He tried not to panic. After all, this was part of his plan. All this time, he'd tried to find a way to get back inside, and here he was, exactly where he needed to be. What he needed now was patience and focus, and hope that he could handle whatever happened next. He would keep going, as his mother had told him in his dream.

"You've gained weight," a low voice said.

The voice was in his own tongue, and it was familiar. In the darkened lab, he looked to the cage on his left marked Y-92, at the yellow eyes staring back at him, so similar to his own. It couldn't be. And yet, it was.

"Hello, Brother," he replied.

KARA LaREAU is the author of many books for young readers, including *Rise of ZomBert* as well as the Theodor Seuss Geisel Honor Book *The Infamous Ratsos* and its sequels. She is also the author of the Unintentional Adventures of the Bland Sisters series of middle-grade novels. Kara LaReau lives in Providence, Rhode Island.

RYAN ANDREWS is a comics artist and illustrator. He is the illustrator of *Rise of ZomBert* by Kara LaReau and *The Dollar Kids* by Jennifer Richard Jacobson and the author-illustrator of the graphic novel *This Was Our Pact*. Two of his web comics have been nominated for Will Eisner Comic Industry Awards. Ryan Andrews lives in Fukuoka, Japan.